My New Teacher

A Lesbian Instalove Romance

Reba Bale

MY NEW TEACHER

© 2024 by Reba Bale

ALL RIGHTS RESERVED. No portion of this book may be reproduced, scanned, transmitted, downloaded, decompiled, reverse engineered, or stored in or introduced into any information storage retrieval system in any form by any means without express permission from the author or publisher, except as permitted by U.S. copyright law. For permissions contact the publisher at authorrebabale@outlook.com.

Warning: the unauthorized reproduction or distribution of this copyrighted work is illegal. Criminal copyright infringement, including infringement without monetary gain, is investigated by the FBI and is punishable by up to 5 years in prison and a fine of $250,000.

This is a work of fiction. Names, characters, places, and incidents are either the product of the author's imagination or are used fictitiously. Any resemblance to actual persons, living or dead, events, organizations, or locals is entirely coincidental. Trademark names are used editorially with no infringement of the respective owner's trademark. All activities depicted occur between consenting characters 18 years or older who are not blood related.

NO AI TRAINING: Without in any way limiting the author's and publisher's exclusive rights under copyright, any use of this publication to "train" generative artificial intelligence (AI) technologies to generate text is expressly prohibited. The author reserves all rights to license uses of this work for generative AI training and development of machine learning language models.

Cover by Paper or Pixels

Contents

1.	About This Book	1
2.	Author's Note	3
3.	Join Reba Bale's Newsletter	4
4.	Dedication	5
5.	Prologue -- Adrianna	6
6.	Erin	11
7.	Adrianna	18
8.	Erin	24
9.	Adrianna	31
10.	Erin	38
11.	Adrianna	45
12.	Erin	51

13. Adrianna	57
14. Erin	64
15. Adrianna	70
16. Erin	76
17. Adrianna	82
18. Erin	89
19. Adrianna	95
20. Erin	101
21. Epilogue – Adrianna	107
22. Special Preview of The Divorcee's First Time	111
23. Other Books by Reba Bale	118
24. About Reba Bale	123

About This Book

She went back to school to find herself after her divorce – instead she found love with a woman.

When Adrianna finally gets the courage to divorce her cheating husband, it's a chance for a fresh start. Married too young to a man who controlled her every move, she can finally pursue her dream of being a photographer and traveling the world. She gets a scholarship to Seattle City College's photography program, and at thirty-five, she goes back to school.

Single mother Erin has a lot on her plate. Between raising her daughter, taking care of her temperamental old house, and juggling three jobs, there's not a lot of time for a personal life. That's never been a problem, until she meets her new photography student. Adrianna is different from her other students. She's smart, engaged, and makes Erin feel things she hasn't felt for a very long time.

There are a million reasons a relationship wouldn't work – their teacher student relationship, their age gap, their very different backgrounds, and the fact Adrianna has never been with a woman before. Erin's already been a relationship tutor for a new lesbian, and there's no way she's going there again. Except as the two women become friends, their differences fall away and all that's left is passion. And maybe love...

"My New Teacher" is book fifteen in the "Friends to Lovers" romantic novella series. Each book in the series is a steamy WLW standalone featuring an LGBTQ couple making the leap from friends to lovers and looking for their "happily ever after".

Be sure to check out a free preview of Reba Bale's lesbian romance "The Divorcee's First Time" at the end of this book!

Author's Note

This book contains several non-detailed references to past domestic violence. If these brief references will be upsetting for you, please skip this book.

By conservative estimates, more than twenty-five percent of women and female-identified individuals will be in an unsafe relationship at some point in their lives. If you or someone you love is experiencing physical, mental, or emotional abuse from an intimate partner, help is available. For information and resources, contact the National Domestic Violence Hotline at https://www.thehotline.org/.

JOIN REBA BALE'S NEWSLETTER

Want a free book? Join my weekly newsletter and you'll receive a fun subscriber gift. I promise I will only email you when there are new releases, free books, or special sales you'll want to see.

Visit my newsletter sign-up page at https://books.rebabale.com/lesbianromance to join today.

DEDICATION

For everyone who's been hurt in some way by an intimate partner. Love should never hurt.

PROLOGUE -- ADRIANNA

"How are you feeling, sis?"

My sister Jasmine looked at me across the box-strewn living room of my brand new one-bedroom apartment, her gaze assessing. I'd been through a lot the last fifteen years, yet my sister had always been there for me, even when I'd tried to push her away. I appreciated it more than I could ever tell her.

"I'm good actually. Looking forward to my next chapter."

"What is your next chapter?" she asked. "Have you decided what you're going to do next?"

"Well, with my share of the house sale and the two years of alimony that the court awarded me, I've got a lot of options."

Having a lot of options was as new to me as sharing my ideas.

"I want to go back to school and learn photography, like I always dreamed about."

Jasmine gave me a smile. "I remember you talking about that when you were younger. How you were going to become a famous photographer and travel the world taking pictures."

"I figure it's not too late. In fact, I got accepted to the arts and photography program at Seattle City College. I got a partial scholarship too," I said proudly.

"You did? That's great!"

My sister rushed over and pulled me into a tight hug.

"I'm so proud of you. I know none of this was easy, but in the end, you're going to be so much happier. I've got to head out, but call me if you need anything, anything at all, you hear?"

"Yes ma'am," I teased.

"And you're coming over for dinner tomorrow. I won't take no for an answer. Come by around six. Hopefully

Grace will be there, and you can meet her too. She's super cool."

My sister had met a woman named Grace at her divorce support group and invited the woman to be her roommate. It was the most impulsive thing my cautious sister had ever done. Apparently Grace's ex refused to leave their house until it sold, but Grace hadn't been able to afford a new place without the house sale happening first. Now she was renting a room at my sister's house. I was pretty sure that my sister had a crush on her new roommate, but of course she denied it.

"Okay, thanks again, Jas. I'll see you tomorrow."

As my sister bustled out of the apartment I looked around with pride. This place was all mine. I could do whatever I wanted in here. Add throw pillows to the couch. Hang a Monet print on the wall. Have plants or a cat, or plants and a cat. All things my husband, now ex-husband, had hated.

The problems in my marriage came on gradually. When I first met Don I was young and naïve, fresh out of high school. Ten years older than me, he was charming and generous and when he told me that he loved me on our second date, I believed we were living out some instalove romantic comedy. My family was concerned about how fast things were moving, but I was too in love to listen.

At first I thought Don was just a little Type A. He always had to have everything in the house just so, something I wrote off as him being quirky. Gradually he isolated me from my friends and tried his best to limit my contact with my family. When he told me he wanted me to quit my job and try for a family, I happily agreed, set on becoming the perfect homemaker and mom. Then he controlled all the money. And soon, he controlled everything about my life.

The verbal abuse started early, but it took a few years before the physical side started. The first time he hit me he cried with his head in my lap, promising that it would never happen again. It did, and I stayed, half convinced that I deserved it and too embarrassed to tell anyone.

Then I found out about the cheating. While Don was controlling my every move, he was also carrying on a long affair with his administrative assistant. He was the very definition of a cliché. I started hiding money and secretly seeing a counselor. I'd seen enough movies to know I needed to plan my exit carefully.

The day I accidentally found out that Don had a vasectomy was the last straw. For years he'd insisted I stay home so we could have a child, but it was really just another way to keep me isolated and under his thumb. All those months I'd been disappointed when my period came, wondering what was wrong with me that I couldn't get pregnant... I'd packed up and left before he returned home from work.

I was smart enough to not go to my family. I knew that was the first place he'd look. Thanks to a friend of my sister I got a space in a shelter for survivors of domestic violence, and I stayed there for nearly a year. They helped me get a restraining order, separate my finances, and find a divorce lawyer.

Now I was finally free. Don had kept me down for years, but now I was back and ready to live life on my own terms. I'd never been so excited. Or scared. But I was ready for the challenge.

I searched around for the bag I'd brought in from the car. It was a large silk screen of a phoenix rising from the ashes. It matched the tattoo I'd gotten on my thigh the day my divorce was final. I was going to hang that right over my bed where I'd see it every day.

I looked around with a smile. Everything was going to be okay now.

Erin

"Mom, do you know where my purple sweater is?"

I looked up from making lunches as I heard my eight year old daughter call down the stairs. It was the first day of school for both of us, and I needed her to move along so we wouldn't be late.

"Which purple sweater?" I called back. "You have like five of them."

I didn't bother to ask why she wanted to wear a sweater when it was already sixty-five degrees outside with a forecast for a hot and sunny day. Summer had come late to Seattle this year, and it was clearly planning to hang on for a while. I had no complaints about that.

"The one with the princesses on it."

One of the mysteries of life was how I'd ended up with a daughter who was obsessed with Disney princesses. She certainly hadn't gotten that from me. And given that her father wasn't around, he couldn't be the source of this extreme girliness.

"It's hanging on the sweater rack in the laundry room."

A few seconds later, Flora ran into the kitchen, wearing a short red skirt, bright yellow boots, and a blue halter top.

"You might want to wear a regular shirt under your sweater in case you decide to take off your sweater in school," I said as she headed for the laundry room. "It's supposed to be warm today. There's no rain predicted either."

When Flora came back from the laundry room she'd changed into denim shorts and a short sleeve green shirt with a butterfly pattern. She was still wearing rain boots. Her purple princess sweater was in her hand. I watched as she shoved it into her Elsa backpack.

"What are we having for lunch?" she asked.

"Leftover pasta salad and turkey sandwiches," I said. "Plus carrot sticks and an apple."

She grimaced to show her displeasure, but didn't complain. She knew better.

"Mama the faucet in the bathroom is leaking more now, I could hear it in my bedroom last night. It made me hafta pee."

"Okay honey, I'll get it fixed as soon as I can."

As soon as I could afford to get a plumber, that was. I had no idea how to replace the faucet or whatever needed to happen. Maybe I'd been crazy to buy this old house. It had been labeled a fixer upper so I knew it would have issues, but I'd been swayed by its charming bones, the large, fenced in backyard, and the fact that it was in the neighborhood with the second best grade school in the county.

We might not have a lot of money, but I was determined to give my daughter the best life I could. It wasn't easy being a single mom, but fortunately I was close with my family, and they helped me a lot, although I tried not to take advantage of their kindness.

Between Flora and my three jobs, I didn't have time for much else. If I got a little lonely from time to time, well, that was the price I had to pay.

Flora was the product of an ill-advised experiment. I'd dated boys in high school, but once I got to college I realized I was a lesbian. After having one bad relationship after another, I started wondering if maybe I should try being with a man again. After all, sexuality was a spectrum, I reasoned. Occasionally I found a man attractive, so maybe I was on the 'mostly lesbian' side of bisexual.

I was drowning my sorrows at a bar near the convention center when I met Flora's father. My most recent girlfriend had just dumped me out of the blue at a restaurant up the street, so I was feeling vulnerable. The man was tall and handsome and only in town for three days for a conference.

When he asked me to go back to his hotel, I figured why not. He was attractive and I was suddenly single. We agreed to not share names. After an unsatisfying sexual encounter – for me anyway -- I slipped out while he was still sleeping.

Eight weeks later I realized I was pregnant. We'd used a condom, but it must have failed. I didn't know the guy's name. Didn't know where he lived or worked. I didn't even remember what hotel room he was in, not that the hotel would have given me any personal information about him even if I had.

With no way to contact him to let him know, I debated my options. I was thirty-five years old and single, pregnant by a stranger. I'd always wanted kids though and realizing that it was probably the only chance I'd have to carry a child, I decided to keep the baby.

And I was glad I had. Most days anyway.

"Are you ready to go, Flora-bell?" I asked, handing her a microwave breakfast burrito she could eat in the car.

"Yes Mommy."

I dropped Flora off at school, then headed towards Seattle City College. One of my three jobs was as an adjunct professor in the art department. I loved teaching, and the college paid a good wage, so I was hoping to get on as a regular faculty member this year. That would mean yearly contracts, higher pay, and benefits. My daughter had health insurance through the state, but I lived in fear of needing to go to the doctor and not being able to afford it.

My first class today was Intro to Photography. It was a required class for photography students, even though it was too remedial for most of them, to ensure that they had all the basics down before they moved onto the more challenging classes. Many art majors also took the class as one of their electives.

I had just enough time to take a few sips of coffee from my thermos before I had to teach. As I walked into my classroom I looked at my students scattered around the tables set up across the room. There were twenty students signed up this semester. Several of them looked bored already and I hadn't even started talking. I suppressed a sigh. I knew from past experience that half of them intended to use their camera phones to skate by even though part of their testing would be on the functions of a real camera.

My eyes caught on a woman sitting in the front row. She was at least ten years older than the rest of the students, probably in her early thirties. She had long black hair, straight and sleek, a wide mouth with sensuous looking pink lips, light brown skin, and dark brown eyes. She was lean but curvy, and while she was dressed in jeans and a tee shirt like pretty much everyone else in class, she somehow looked sophisticated.

The woman must have felt me studying her because she looked up and gave me a small smile. Our eyes met and held for a few seconds longer than appropriate before I pulled myself together and looked away. My mind was racing with the realization that I was attracted to this woman. I'd never been attracted to a student before, and I couldn't start now. The last thing I needed was to lose my job.

Taking a deep breath, I turned to face the classroom again, leaning against my desk as my eyes moved from one side of the room to the other.

"Good morning everyone, my name is Erin Robbins, and I'll be your instructor for this class."

Adrianna

My photography instructor was hot. Her dark hair was curly, framing her heart shaped face. She didn't appear to be wearing any make-up, but she didn't need it. She was a natural beauty. I studied her, trying to assess her age. Around forty I guessed, based on the fine lines forming in the corners of her eyes and around her mouth when she smiled.

Erin Robbins was curvy, something highlighted by the pencil skirt she wore with a short sleeve blouse tucked into the waistband. Her legs were shapely, telling me she either worked out or spent a lot of time on her feet.

I paid close attention as our instructor reviewed the syllabus. I could already tell that she wouldn't be the soft touch that I was sure some of these young freshmen were hoping for. It was only my second day on campus, and I could already tell that I was going to be the oldest person in all of my classes. This was a commuter college, and it seemed to mostly attract kids fresh out of high school looking to get their associates degree before moving onto one of the universities for their bachelor's degrees.

When class was over I stayed after to ask a question.

"Um, Professor Robbins?" I said to get her attention. "May I ask you a question?"

She turned, giving me a small smile. She really was quite beautiful.

"You can call me Erin. What's your name?"

I got momentarily sidetracked. It had been a while since I was in school, but teachers never wanted to be called by their first name. Then again, I guess that college was a little different.

"My name is Adrianna."

"It's nice to meet you Adrianna, are you a freshman?" Erin gave me another smile that made her eyes crinkle.

"Yes, I took a little sabbatical between high school and college, like seventeen years," I joked. "I was just wondering if you had any recommendations for a camera? I have this one, but it's kind of old. I was wondering if you think I should buy a newer one?"

I pulled out a Nikon camera I'd purchased at an estate sale about two years ago. I wasn't even totally sure how to use it, to be honest. I didn't know what all the buttons were for or how to choose on the lenses that came with it, but I knew from the syllabus that we'd reviewed today that we'd be learning all of that and more.

As I handed the camera to Erin, our hands brushed against each other. My breath caught as I felt a little tingle where our skin touched. Erin's eyes shot down to look at our hands, telling me that whatever it was, she felt it too.

"Whoa, this is a really nice camera," Erin said, pulling away and turning it over in her hands.

"It is?" I asked. "I have to confess that even though I've always been interested in photography, I know nothing about cameras. That's why I'm excited to take your class."

"This is a three thousand dollar camera," she told me. "And you have at least a thousand dollars' worth of accessories in this bag."

"Holy crap. I paid fifty bucks for it at an estate sale." I shook my head. "I guess someone's kids didn't know what they had there."

"That was a lucky find then," Erin told me. "You'll do just fine with this. I guarantee you that no one else in class will have a professional camera like this. Did the owner's manual come in the bag?"

"No."

"Well Nikon has them all online," she told me. "I recommend looking up this model and printing it out so you can become familiar with all the features."

"I will, thank you."

I put the camera back into its bag carefully, remembering the day I bought it and hid it in the back of my closet behind our old suitcases, afraid my husband would be pissed that I'd bought it. Who knew it was such a good find?

"See you on Thursday," Erin said, packing up her tote bag.

I headed to my next class, then stopped at the bookstore to pick up some textbooks before heading home.

The next month passed quickly. I loved all my classes, but my photography class with Erin was my favorite. I looked forward to Tuesday and Thursday mornings the whole rest of the week. She was such a good teacher – entertaining, knowledgeable, and patient, even with the eighteen year olds who were clearly only taking the class to knock off what they thought would be an easy elective.

I found myself coming up with excuses to stay after class and talk to Erin. I felt drawn to her, but I couldn't say why really. Until the night I had a dream about her. In the dream, we were in the kitchen at my house and suddenly she was naked. I laid her out on my kitchen island and started licking her pussy, my fingers gripping her milky white thighs until I left marks. Finally Erin cried out, her back arching, as she shuddered through an orgasm. And when Dream Me lifted my head, Erin's cream was all over my mouth and chin.

I woke up with my heart pounding and my panties soaked. Had I just had a sex dream about my teacher?

I stared at the ceiling in confusion. I'd always assumed that I was firmly on Team Hetero, but then again it wasn't like I'd had a lot of experience with dating or relationships. I'd dated one boy in high school and then met my husband the summer after high school graduation. It wasn't like I'd had time to experiment and learn what I liked.

After that dream I started paying more attention to the people around me, noting what features I found attractive and imagining myself kissing them or touching them to see how my body reacted. Unfortunately, my teacher Erin was the only person I seemed to have a positive reaction to, which only made me more confused.

Not that it mattered if I was attracted to her. She was my teacher. There was no way we could be together anyway.

Erin

"Damn it!"

I popped the hood of my car, going back out into the pouring rain to stare at the engine as if I knew anything about how to fix my car. Shielding my phone with my raincoat, I called my mother's number and then my father's before remembering that they'd gone out of town for a long weekend.

I debated my options. I needed to pick up Flora from her after school program. They charged twenty bucks for every minute you were late, something I couldn't afford, especially with what was likely an expensive car repair. I pulled up my Uber app. Between the storm and it being rush hour, it was surge pricing right now. And payday wasn't until next week.

I punched my hands up at the sky, cursing the world. Why couldn't I just get a damned break?

I was so busy ranting at the sky that I didn't notice that a car had pulled up next to me until I heard my name.

"Erin? Is that you? Is everything okay?"

Oh my God, I was so upset I'd totally forgotten that I was still in the college's parking lot where I might run into a student. And of course it was Adrianna, the woman I had a very inappropriate crush on. Fuck my life.

I took a deep breath and walked closer to her car, water pouring over the hood of my raincoat.

"Oh hey Adrianna. Yeah, I'm fine."

She looked skeptical. "Is your car dead?"

"Yeah."

"Is it the battery?" she asked. "I have jumper cables."

I shook my head. "No, the battery is working. I think it's the starter or something else. I'm going to have to get it towed."

I wondered silently if the college would be okay if I left it there until next week when I could afford to get it towed.

I was a forty-three year old woman. How was I still living like this?

"Hop in, I'll give you a ride," Adrianna said, pulling me out of my self-flagellation.

"Oh no, I can call an Uber or something," I replied, wondering if there was a bus between here and Flora's daycare.

"Erin." Adrianna's voice sounded exasperated. "It's pouring out. You'll never get an Uber right now. I'm glad to give you a ride, honestly."

Realizing I was out of options, I acquiesced. "That would be great, thanks."

I grabbed my bag and Flora's car seat from the car, locked the door, and walked over to the passenger side of Adrianna's car. It was an older model Lexus, way more expensive than I could ever afford.

"Sorry, I'm going to get water all over your car," I said as I slid into the seat.

"I'll turn on the seat warmer, it'll dry you off," Adrianna said cheerfully. "Where to?"

"If you wouldn't mind, could you drop me off at my daughter's after school program? It's at Tubman Elementary School."

"I know right where that is," she said, putting the car in drive and pulling out of her parking space.

We were both quiet for a few minutes before she asked, "How old is your daughter?"

"She's eight," I said.

I wiggled a little as the heat from the seat started seeping through my bottom. It felt nice.

"I'm a single mom," I added, wanting her to know I wasn't married. I couldn't say why. Adrianna was straight, I knew this because in one of our conversations she'd mentioned recently divorcing her husband.

"That sounds hard," she said sympathetically.

I blinked quickly as tears pricked against my eyes. It was nice for someone to acknowledge that every now and then.

Twelve minutes later we pulled up to Flora's school.

"Thanks so much for the ride Adrianna, I appreciate it."

"Wait," she said, her hand coming to my forearm.

I swear I could feel the heat of her touch despite a heavy raincoat and long sleeve shirt between us.

"Go get your daughter," she said. "I'll drive you two home."

"Oh, I couldn't impose…," my words broke off as I imagined Flora and I standing in the pouring rain waiting for a bus home.

"It's not an imposition," she said firmly. "I'll wait here."

I hurried inside the building, finding Flora already wearing her coat and waiting for me near the door. A quick look around told me that she was the last kid to be picked up. I reminded myself that I'd gotten here as soon as I could. Thank God for Adrianna offering me a ride, otherwise I don't know what I would have done.

"Hey Flora-bell, we're getting a ride with my friend today." I grabbed her hand and started walking towards the door.

"How come?" she asked.

"My car broke down."

"You need to buy a new one, Mommy," she said, as if it was that simple.

"We can't afford a new car right now," I said, rushing her towards Adrianna's car. I was already wondering if I could pick up extra shifts at one of my jobs to help pay for the car repairs.

The rain had slowed down in the few minutes I'd been inside, but it was still raining steadily. I opened the back door and to my surprise, Adrianna had already installed Flora's car seat. She was tall enough that she just needed the booster version. I made quick work of buckling her in, then closed the door and got into the front seat.

"Flora, this is Miss Adrianna."

"Hi, I'm Flora, I'm eight."

Adrianna smiled at her. "Hi Flora, it's nice to meet you."

"You got any food in this car?" Flora asked.

Adrianna shook her head. "No, I'm sorry, I don't."

Flora sighed in disappointment. "I'm starving!"

I resisted rolling my eyes, knowing that they'd served her a snack after school.

"We'll be home soon, sweetie," I reminded her.

My daughter sighed again dramatically, making Adrianna smile. "I'll get you home before you pass out from hunger, don't worry."

ADRIANNA

Little Flora was adorable. She looked like a miniature version of her mother, with long curly dark hair and huge brown eyes. And those bright yellow rain boots she was wearing were so cute.

"What are we havin' for dinner, Mommy?" Flora asked as we pulled away from the school.

"Um. I don't know, I have to see what we have in the fridge," Erin replied.

"I want pizza."

"We don't have pizza," Erin said.

"But I want it!"

Erin sent me an apologetic look.

"Sorry," she said quietly. "She gets a little whiny when she's tired."

"I'm the same way," I reassured her with a wink.

It took about ten minutes before we arrived at a large Victorian house. It looked like it had seen better days, but the yard was tidy.

"Thanks again," Erin said as she unbuckled her seatbelt. "You really saved me today."

"It really was no problem."

I waited while she helped Flora out of the car and retrieved the booster seat.

"Bye Miss Adrianna," Flora called as she exited.

I smiled as she stumbled a bit on my name. It was a mouthful.

"Goodbye Flora, it was nice to meet you."

As I started to back out of the driveway I could hear Flora complaining loudly about wanting pizza. It gave me an idea. Would it be too forward of me? After a quick internal debate, I called my favorite pizza place. My friend Amy, the owner of the shop, answered the phone.

"Oh hey Adrianna, you want some pizza?"

"Yeah but I'm not sure what to order," I said. "It's for an eight year old."

"Tell you what, I just had an order canceled. I've got three large pies here, one vegetarian, one taco, and one pepperoni. Come pick them up and they're yours, on the house."

Amy's shop was only a little more than a mile away. I popped inside to grab the pizza, thanking my friend profusely, then headed back to Erin's house. Hoping I was doing the right thing, I rang the doorbell. A minute later Erin appeared in the doorway, Flora by her side.

"Adrianna," Erin looked confused to see me.

"I hope I'm not overstepping but…it seemed like you were having a bad day, so here." I handed her the stack of pizza boxes.

"You brought pizza?" Erin said, looking confused.

"Yay pizza!" Flora was jumping up and down on her toes excitedly.

"I can't take these," Erin said. "This must be seventy-five bucks worth of pizza."

Two things were becoming apparent to me. Erin was struggling financially, and she was too stubborn to accept help. I had no debt and a nice settlement from the divorce, so I was determined to help.

"Mommy!" Flora said loudly. "I want the pizza! It smells so good."

"My friend owns the pizza shop," I said hurriedly. "They were from a canceled order. She gave them to me for free. Please, take them."

When I pushed the boxes towards Erin she took them automatically, still looking reluctant.

"Enjoy your pizza."

As I started to walk away Erin called out, "Wait. At least join us for dinner."

Erin's house was clean but a bit chaotic, the way houses with kids tended to be. The dining room table was covered with one of Flora's art projects, so the three of us ate in the kitchen. Erin and I drank beer with our pizza while Flora drank a sparkling water.

The little girl had never had taco pizza before and soon declared, "This is the best pizza ever!" to both of our amusement.

After dinner Flora headed off for her one hour of screen time while Erin and I sat talking at the table. It was nice, a level of domesticity that I never remembered having with my husband.

"Do you mind if I ask about her father?" I nodded towards the living room where cartoon characters were singing on the screen.

"One night stand," Erin said, giving me a look that said I'd better not be judging her. "I was trying to convince myself that I wasn't a lesbian."

I started choking on my beer. "What? Why?"

"I'd had one bad relationship after another. I'd just gotten dumped by my girlfriend, and this guy started flirting with me at a bar and I thought, maybe being with guys wouldn't be that bad."

"And was it?"

She nodded. "Oh yeah. I doubt the dude even noticed I was there before he fell asleep."

We both laughed.

"My sister is a lesbian," I said. "She recently divorced her partner so she's having a hard time."

"Oh, that's too bad. So you both got divorced recently?"

"Yeah."

For some reason I hadn't thought about the way my sister and I had been on similar trajectories in terms of relationships. Probably because Jasmine always seemed so calm and settled. I wondered if she was hiding some of her stronger emotions from me.

"I guess I should go," I said, popping out of my chair.

Erin stood up at the same time, turning to face me. We were only a few inches apart, and both of us froze. As I stared into Erin's dark eyes I felt a hum of what could only be attraction. I had the strongest urge to reach forward and kiss her, which was crazy. I was here to be a friend to her, not hit on her. Not to mention that I'd have no idea what to do with a woman anyway.

I took a deep breath and stepped back.

"See you in class."

When I turned back Erin was still standing by the table, looking confused.

Erin

I wasn't sure what to make of my encounter with Adrianna. She'd saved me from draining the last of my bank account on Uber surge pricing and given me and my kid a warm dry ride home. But bringing the pizza... that was next level thoughtful. It was good pizza too.

There was something in her expression when I'd opened the door and found her standing on the front porch. It was almost like she was nervous that I was going to yell at her or something. I couldn't say why.

The pizza had saved me almost as much as the ride. When I'd picked up Flora from after school care she'd been cranky as hell. I knew from past experience that her mood would have continued to deteriorate as I'd made dinner out of the meager contents of our refrigerator.

Those three pizzas not only gave us dinner Thursday night, but there was more than enough for me to serve for lunch and dinner on Friday.

Since my parents were gone for the weekend I didn't take any catering shifts. Flora usually slept over at their house on Saturdays so I could pick up some extra money. A friend had a catering company, and she almost always had a wedding or some other event on Saturdays. The pay was good, and the tips were even better. It was a good way to supplement my income from the college and my part-time job at a bookstore.

The weather was still rainy, so Flora and I spent a nice Saturday at home, doing craft projects. I framed and matted some photographs to put up on my Etsy store, and the two of us worked to give the entire house a good cleaning. It was a good day, but Adrianna was never far from my mind.

She wasn't far from Flora's mind either. My little girl was quite taken with Adrianna, and kept bringing her up asking when we would see her again. So much so that I thought we'd both hallucinated when we saw her again.

On Sunday we decided to take the bus down to Pike's Place Market to look around. The large open air market was a huge tourist attraction, but it was something that always entertained my daughter as well.

"I want to see the men throwing fish, Mommy."

We were standing in front of the Fish Market watching employees toss freshly caught fish around – hamming it up for Flora's benefit – when I heard someone call my name.

Adrianna was there with another woman who looked enough like her that I knew immediately she was a relative.

"Oh hey Adrianna."

Flora tore her attention away from the fish long enough to fling herself at my student.

"Miss Adrianna. Did you come to watch the fish?"

"I sure did," she said, smiling at me over my daughter's head.

"Hi, I'm Adrianna's sister Jasmine," the other woman said, reaching out to shake my hand. "I've heard so much about you, Erin. And you too, Flora."

Adrianna shot her a look that clearly said, 'shut up'.

"Adrianna just loves your class," she continued, exchanging another look with her sister.

"She's a great student," I said honestly.

Adrianna was progressing nicely in my class. She had a natural eye for composition and lighting, and with me teaching her how to use her fancy camera, she was already taking incredible photographs.

The four of us wandered the length of the market together, Flora chattering nonstop and soaking up the attention of two people who weren't me. As we neared the exit, my phone rang.

"Erin, thank God you picked up." My friend Gail's voice sounded frantic. "I've got three people out with COVID for this big retirement party today. Is there any way you can come in?"

"Oh Gail, I'm so sorry, but my parents are out of town this weekend, so I don't have childcare for Flora. I really wish I could help. Also my car is broken."

"I'll order you an Uber on my account," Gail said. "You can bring Flora. She can play games in the kitchen or something. Please, I'll pay you double."

My eyes shifted to Flora who was listening carefully. "What's happening, Mommy?"

"Hold on one sec, Gail." I placed my hand over the speaker. "Aunt Gail wants me to work today."

"You have another job?" Adrianna asked curiously.

I'd almost forgotten she and Jasmine were here with Gail's panic. My friend was normally very stoic.

"Yeah, I work in a bookstore and also do catering service sometimes on the weekends for extra money."

"I can go home with Miss Adrianna so you can help Aunt Gail," Flora announced.

My eyes widened. "Oh no Flora, it's not polite to just invite yourself over to people's houses like that. Aunt Gail suggested that you come with me."

"It's okay Erin," Adrianna said. "I don't mind babysitting for a while. Then you can focus on your job."

"But..."

"Mommy, you said you needed money to fix the car."

My cheeks flamed with embarrassment, and Adrianna put her hand on my arm.

"Honestly, we'll be fine, I promise. I'd love to hang out with Flora." She pulled out her phone. "Give me your phone number. I'll text you so you have mine."

I hesitated for another few seconds. I really needed the money, and Gail never asked for favors like this, so I knew she was desperate. I'd gotten to know Adrianna over the last couple of months and while I wouldn't say I knew her well, my instincts told me I could trust her.

I rattled off my phone number and watched as Adrianna texted me a picture of her driver's license.

"So you have my address," she winked, but I knew she was also telling me that I could trust her.

"Are you sure you don't mind?" I asked.

"I don't mind at all," Adrianna assured me. "Jasmine and I were going to go out to dinner after this, then we'll head to my apartment. Is there anything I need to know? Allergies? Medical conditions? Phobias?"

I shook my head. "None that we know of."

"Well great, it's settled then." She looked down at my daughter who was wearing a big smile. "What would you like for dinner, Miss Flora?"

"Pie!"

"Flora!" I scolded.

"Fine," Flora said sullenly. "I want to eat with chopsticks then."

Adrianna and Jasmine rolled their lips in to avoid laughing, looking almost like twins.

"Okay, let's go to Jasmine's favorite Chinese restaurant, then we'll see about dessert."

"You listen to Miss Adrianna and Miss Jasmine," I told Flora. "No running off. No talking back. No temper tantrums. No whining."

Flora rolled her eyes. "I know Mom. I'm not a baby."

And then my baby walked off, her hand clasping Adrianna's. I hoped I was making the right decision trusting Adrianna with my kid. I picked up the phone again.

"Okay Gail, I can come in. Send the Uber to the front door of Pike Place."

Adrianna

By the time Jasmine dropped me and Flora off at my apartment we were both stuffed. Since Flora wasn't sure what she liked, we'd ordered half the menu, boxing the rest up for Flora to bring home. The little girl had been thrilled to bring leftovers home for her mother.

After that we'd walked down to a dessert shop and ordered pie. Jasmine and I both ordered apple a la mode while Flora went with peanut butter chocolate cream. I had a feeling that it was more than her mother would have allowed her to order, but she'd eaten a fair amount of vegetables with dinner so I figured a little extra sugar wouldn't hurt her. We also purchased a piece of cherry pie to go for Erin.

"This is my apartment," I told Flora as I opened the door after Jasmine dropped us off. I knew Jas was dying to ask me questions about Erin but had refrained around her daughter.

Flora charged in, looking around curiously. "It's smaller than my house," she observed with the honesty of a young child.

"It is, but I still like it."

After putting our leftovers in the refrigerator, I pulled out an extra toothbrush so Flora could brush her teeth, then gave her a bottle of water to drink.

Erin had already texted once to check on Flora, so I took a selfie of the two of us holding up our water bottles and sent it to her with a message that we'd made it back to my apartment safely.

Erin responded with a thumbs up a few minutes later.

During the course of our conversation earlier Flora had learned that I'd never seen *Frozen* before, so she was determined to fix that. I found it on a streaming service, and we settled down on the couch to watch it. Fifteen minutes later she was sound asleep, no doubt crashing from the sugar overload.

She was adorable. I watched the end of *Frozen* just to say that I did, then sent Erin a picture of her daughter sleeping on the couch.

"I'll be done in about an hour," she wrote back.

When Erin got to my place it was already nine o'clock. She looked exhausted.

"Thank you so much," she said as soon as I opened the door.

"It's no problem, we had fun." I pointed to where Flora was still sound asleep on the couch. "She's been sleeping for a while. Did you eat?"

She shook her head. "I was too busy."

I was overwhelmed with the urge to take care of her, although I couldn't say why.

"Come into the kitchen, we have leftover Chinese food."

She seemed conflicted. "I should probably go, we've bothered you enough for one day."

"Nonsense, come into the kitchen," I ordered.

I knew Erin was tired because she followed my instructions without argument. I brought her a bottle of water, a plate, and the bag of Chinese food.

"Help yourself, we can heat it up in the microwave."

Erin's eyes widened comically. "Um, did you order everything on the menu?"

I laughed. "Flora couldn't tell us what she liked so we ordered anything that had something she liked as an ingredient. We told her she could take the rest home, and she said you would be happy to have dinner."

"My kid is very thoughtful," she said as she started filling a plate.

Once she had a variety I stuck the plate in the microwave and offered her a beer, opening one for her and one for me.

"How was work?"

"It was crazy busy. We were down to two people, and it was a particularly demanding group."

We chatted easily while Erin ate her dinner and by the time she was done, her head was drooping.

"I should wake up Flora and get an Uber."

"Why don't you sleep over?" I asked impulsively. "There's no sense waking up Flora, and you're ready to drop."

"I…"

I held up my hand. "Don't argue with me Erin. You can't go home like this, and your daughter is sleeping peacefully. Come on, I'll set you two up in my guest room."

I showed Erin around, then offered her a pair of pajama pants and a tee shirt to sleep in. Once she had changed and used the restroom, she picked up Flora and carried her into the guest room. I followed behind, bringing them an extra blanket. I set it on the bottom of the bed and then turned to say goodnight. Erin was staring at me, a bemused look on her face.

"You've been very kind, Adrianna," she said quietly. "It's, well it's not easy for me to accept help, so thank you."

"It's no problem," I replied softly. "I'd like to think that we're becoming friends."

She nodded. "I guess we are."

"The semester is over in a few weeks," I reminded her. "Maybe we can hang out some time."

"I'd like that."

Impulsively I pulled Erin into a hug. It felt incredible to have her in my arms, even for just a moment, and when she wrapped her arms around me too it made me realize the truth. I was attracted to her, no matter how impossible it was. I pulled away, avoiding her gaze.

"Good night."

As soon as I got into bed I texted my sister.

> **Adrianna:** *How did you figure out you were a lesbian?*

> **Jasmine:** *I knew it! I knew there was a vibe between you and Erin. Call me right now.*

> **Adrianna:** *I can't. Erin and Flora are sleeping over. In the guest room. The walls are very thin here.*

> **Jasmine:** *Come over for dinner tomorrow. I want to hear everything.*

Erin

After the night Flora and I slept over at her house, Adrianna and I started texting each other. At first it was a couple of texts here and there, but within a week it was multiple times a day. In the evenings after Flora went to bed we'd have long conversations, getting to know each other, talking about our days, and sharing our hopes and dreams.

By unspoken agreement, we avoided any extra contact on campus, but we met for coffee twice near my house, and she joined us for dinner at Flora's favorite restaurant -- the Spaghetti House -- one night at my daughter's insistence.

It was great seeing the two of them together. Flora seemed quite smitten with Adrianna, kind of like her mother, and for her part, Adrianna seemed to like Flora just as much.

The whole situation was confusing. I knew that Adrianna had been married to a man for years and while that didn't preclude her being bisexual, she never mentioned dating a woman. It was ridiculous for me to have a crush on a hetero, but there it was.

Of course sexual orientation wasn't our only difference. I was her teacher, although that was only for a short while longer. I was also eight years older than her, and an overworked and overstressed single mom. I hadn't done much more than the occasional hook-up since Flora was born. I had no idea how to date as a mom, even if Adrianna were gay.

I'd dated someone who wanted to experiment with being a lesbian years ago, and it hadn't ended well. After that I vowed that I'd never date anyone who was bicurious again. I told myself that Adrianna and I were just friends, and that's all we'd ever been, even while my traitorous heart told me the truth: I was falling in love with her.

In fact, I'd fallen for her the instant I saw her.

The semester ended and I posted everyone's grade. Fortunately, the class had a pass/fail grading option and Adrianna, like pretty much every student, had chosen that option. If anyone ever questioned whether she got any preferential treatment from me, it would be much easier to defend a simple 'pass' versus an 'A'. And make no mistake, Adrianna would have gotten an 'A'. Not because I had feelings for her, but because she was that good. Plus she did all the extra credit work, something that most students skipped.

As I'd gotten to know Adrianna, I'd learned a little bit about her story and understood how major it was for her to finally start the college education that she'd put aside at her husband's insistence all those years ago.

To commemorate finishing her first semester of college, Jasmine was holding a small celebration dinner at a restaurant in Queen Anne. Apparently Jasmine made pretty good money in real estate, and she wanted to do something nice for her sister. There were eight of us who met for dinner, including Adrianna's parents, Jasmine's friend and roommate Grace, and two of Adrianna's friends that she'd recently reconnected with, one of whom was the owner of the pizza shop where we'd gotten pizza that first night.

As we finished up dinner, Jasmine turned to me, her gaze calculating. "Hey Erin, are you in a hurry to get home?"

I shook my head. "No, my parents have Flora tonight."

"Oh great, do you mind giving Adrianna a ride home? Grace and I need to get home and check on our cats."

"We can give you a ride home, Pumpkin," Adrianna's father offered.

"No Dad," Jasmine interrupted. "It's closer for Erin."

She gave her father a look I couldn't interpret, and he backed down. When I turned to Adrianna, she was studying her sister with her eyes narrowed, obviously thinking something was up. If I didn't know better, I would have sworn that Jasmine was trying to be a matchmaker.

And maybe she was, because as she and Grace followed us out of the restaurant she whispered, "You girls have fun."

We were both quiet on the drive back to Adrianna's apartment. It was late enough that traffic was light, and it wasn't long before I was pulling up in front of the building.

"Would you like to come up for a glass of wine or something?" she asked.

I'd only had one beer with dinner, so another drink was safe. "Sure."

As soon as we walked into her apartment, Adrianna turned to face me. "I have a confession to make."

She looked suddenly nervous, which made me nervous. "What?"

She bit her lip, then looked up to meet my gaze. "I, uh, I think I have a crush on you."

I reared back in surprise even while my heart started thudding happily. "You do? I thought you were straight."

"I thought I was too. Until I met you."

I stared at her for a long moment, trying to decide what to say or do next. But Adrianna took the decision out of my hands by moving closer and taking my face between her hands. My skin hummed where she touched me.

"I want to kiss you, is that okay?" Adrianna's voice was barely above a whisper.

"Yeah." I nodded, just to emphasize that I was giving consent.

Adrianna moved in slowly and I stood absolutely still, letting her take the lead. Her lips pressed against mine, softly at first, and then she added some pressure. I fisted my hands at my side, resisting the urge to touch her.

She moved a little closer until only an inch or two separated our bodies, then pressed her tongue against the seam of my lips. I opened my mouth and her tongue slid in tentatively exploring. I slid my tongue against hers, watching her reaction. She must have liked it, because Adrianna deepened the kiss, and pulled me closer. She kissed me until we were both out of breath, then she pulled away. This close I could see the pulse point in her throat beating wildly.

"Holy shit," she said softly, her tone awed, "That was nice."

Adrianna

"Nice? Just nice?" Erin's voice was teasing. "I'll show you nice."

She grabbed my waist and turned me, backing me up until my ass connected with the front door. My heart was racing excitedly. That first kiss had been incredible. I couldn't wait to see what happened next.

I'd had a long conversation with my sister after the night that Erin and Flora slept over at my house. I knew logically that sexuality was a spectrum, but my feelings for Erin still caught me by surprise.

***

"Can you just be a lesbian for one person?" I'd asked Jasmine after I confessed that I was crushing on Erin.

"Well, I'm not the person who makes the rules, but think of it this way. Have you ever seen a man who you found attractive and thought, well he's not my type but I really find him attractive?"

"You mean like both of the guys I dated were dark haired, but I had a secret crush on my nerdy Scandinavian science teacher in high school?"

"Yeah. So the thing is, maybe you're a lesbian," Jasmine said. "It's more likely you're bisexual and attracted to only certain kinds of women like you're attracted to different kinds of men. But regardless, you don't need to label it. If you like Erin and you think she likes you, go for it."

***

I took my sister's advice and now I was going for it. And I was damned glad I was when Erin pressed her body against mine and took my mouth in a hard kiss that made my entire body tingle. Her hands slid to my waist, fingers digging into my softness as the kiss went on and on.

"You taste fucking delicious," she growled against my lips before going in for another kiss.

We were similar heights, so our bodies fit together perfectly. Erin was grinding her hips against mine now, the pressure hitting me in just the right spot to ramp up my excitement.

Realizing that I was just standing there passively, I reached around her body, giving into my instinct to touch Erin's ass. She had a great ass, perfectly round and muscled, and when I gave it a little squeeze, Erin groaned against my mouth, making me feel powerful.

My husband was the only man I'd ever done more than just make out with, and even early on in our relationship, it had never been about my pleasure. I'd often thought that it could have been any random woman in his bed and my husband wouldn't notice. If it wasn't for the vibrator that I'd carefully hid from him all the years we were married, I would have thought it was impossible for me to climax.

But pressed between Erin's body and the door I was already more turned on than I'd ever been in my life. And it freaked me out the tiniest bit.

As if Erin felt my sudden attack of nerves, she pulled away, kissing her way down my neck before stepping back. My body mourned the loss of her warmth even as my brain appreciated the reprieve. I'd been prepared to kiss Erin, I just hadn't been prepared to feel so much when it happened.

Erin studied me for a minute before taking another step back.

"I should probably get going before we do something that you're not ready for."

I flinched. "I'm sorry."

Her hand came up slowly to cup my cheek. "You have the right to feel how you feel," she said softly. "I get it, this is new for you, and you're only a year out of a terrible relationship. I'm not mad at you, believe me. Even if I never kiss you again, I'll be masturbating to the memory of that kiss for a long, long time."

She leaned forward and pressed a chaste kiss on my lips.

"I'll talk to you tomorrow."

And then she was walking out the door.

"Text me to let me know you got home okay," I called out the door after her.

That night when I went to bed I fingered myself into the most powerful orgasm I'd had in my life, all the time reliving that kiss with Erin.

The next day Erin invited me to come to dinner. She and Flora had decided on one of their favorite themes – Breakfast for Dinner – and afterwards they were having puzzle night. I took the invitation as a good sign that she wasn't mad at me for freaking out a little when we kissed.

When I got to Erin's house Flora answered the door, throwing herself towards me and hugging my waist. She was wearing purple tights, a pink sparkly skirt, and a plaid shirt, her hair a mess of tangled curls.

"Miss Adrianna! I missed you."

"I missed you too, Flora," I told her sincerely, meeting Erin's eyes over her daughter's head. "But then I heard y'all were having breakfast for dinner and I knew I had to come over."

"If we eat our protein we get to have waffles for dessert," Flora whispered conspiratorially.

At least I think she meant to whisper. The child was a loud talker no matter how much she tried to tone it down.

When I closed the door it bounced back open.

"You've got to put some weight in it," Erin called. "The door is warped."

I followed mother and daughter into the kitchen where they were making omelets. There were breakfast potatoes roasting in the oven with a tray of bacon, and a platter of fruit cut up on the countertop. Flora and I set the dining room table while Erin finished up our food and to my shock I saw Flora bring out wine glasses.

"We're havin' mimosas," she said excitedly.

I exchanged a look with Erin. "Virgin mimosas," she clarified, holding up a bottle of non-alcoholic sparkling juice.

"What are we celebrating?" I asked.

"Mommy sold a set of photographs on Etsy and made lots of money."

"Did she now?" I asked, "I didn't know your mommy did that."

Erin was the hardest working person I knew. Between raising Flora, the three jobs, and now this Etsy side hustle, I was surprised that she had enough time to sleep.

"Not 'lots' of money," Erin clarified. "But enough for us to have a treat. Let me get the bacon, and then we'll have our feast."

As I watched her walk back into the kitchen, I couldn't help thinking that there was something else I'd like to feast on.

It was crazy how much fun I had just eating dinner and putting together a puzzle with Erin and Flora. The mother daughter duo was hilarious together, their bond evident. I'd grown up in a house like this, full of love and laughter, and I hadn't realized how much I'd missed it until I started spending time over here. This was the life I'd dreamed about when I was a starry-eyed teenager, but it had never been possible with my husband.

The whole thing made me sad, but I was resolved not to look back. I could have my dream now. I had a new life, and I was going to enjoy every minute of it, including exploring this attraction between me and the woman who'd become a good friend.

ERIN

"Is she asleep?"

"Finally," I told Adrianna. "We don't have guests over very often. She got overexcited."

"She's a great little girl," Adrianna said.

Her words filled me with maternal pride. "She's everything to me."

"I guess I should go," she said, sounding reluctant.

I shared her reluctance.

"How about a glass of wine before you go?"

"Sounds good," Adrianna replied.

I poured us each a glass and we settled on the couch, mostly silent. I'd noticed that Adrianna wasn't one for pointless small talk, but I could tell that she was distracted tonight. Likely for the same reason I was.

"Should we talk about what happened?" I finally asked.

Adrianna turned to face me, her knees brushing against mine. "I've never kissed a woman before," she said softly. "I don't know what all this means, but that was.... well, it was the best kiss of my life."

I knew the feeling. "I've kissed a lot of women, and it's not always like that. But I need to be honest with you, Adrianna. I've been burned before by someone who was experimenting."

I expected her to brush off my concern, but instead she nodded, clearly considering my words.

"I don't know what's going to happen, Erin. I don't have a lot of experience dating men or women. The only thing I know is that I can't get you out of my mind."

I set my wine glass on the table next to hers and moved forward. Adrianna met me halfway. Our lips touched for an instant, then the kiss turned hot. I shifted to face her more fully, tunneling my fingers in the soft strands of her hair, tilting her face so she was in the perfect position for me to plunder her mouth with my tongue.

Adrianna made a little moaning sound as she scooted closer but given the way we were sitting on the couch, our knees were in the way. Without releasing her mouth, I moved my hands to her shoulders, pushing her down to her back and following her down. I shifted so my body weight was between Adrianna and the back of the couch, then kissed my way down her neck and across her collar bone.

My fingers went to the hem of her shirt, shoving it up underneath her armpits so I could get to her tits. I sucked one nipple into my mouth through the thin fabric of her bra, and Adrianna arched her back, trying to get closer to my questing mouth.

Suddenly she tugged on my hair.

"I want to touch you too," she said, pushing up to a seated position.

I unbuttoned my shirt and opened the front closure of my bra, freeing my breasts. She stared at them almost reverently before reaching out one finger and circling a nipple.

Emboldened, she leaned forward, taking my nipple into her mouth and sucking it carefully.

"You don't have to be gentle," I told her. "Think about what you like and do that. If I don't like it, I'll tell you."

She gave me a quick glance from underneath her eyelashes, then pushed on my sternum. I shifted until I was the one on my back on the couch. She pushed my legs apart enough to slide her hips between my thighs, then lowered herself down until she was draped over me, her mouth right at breast level.

This time when she touched my nipple, she wasn't tentative. She sucked as much as she could into her mouth, adding suction while tapping at the tip with her tongue.

"Yes, Adrianna," I gasped, pressing her head closer, "just like that."

Her other hand snaked up to give my other nipple attention, pulling and pinching until I was ready to come just from that stimulation. When she pulled off, I rolled us so we were side by side on the couch, then scooted down to line up our faces.

This time I let Adrianna be the aggressor in the kiss, and I could feel her grow more confident.

She gasped against my mouth as I shoved my hand between her thighs. My hand stilled.

"Do you want me to stop?" I asked, meeting her gaze.

"Fuck no."

I pressed my hand firmly against her center, caressing her through the fabric of the leggings she was wearing. Her core was hot and damp and I was dying to rip the light coverings off her body and eat her out, but I knew we needed to move slow. This was Adrianna's first time with a woman, and I didn't want to freak her out. For all that I'd said I'd never be with a baby lesbian again, I couldn't help the primal urge I felt to take her and be her first. But I wanted to take care of her too. Needed to take care of her.

Her legs widened enough that I was able to shove the fabric of her crotch in between her pussy lips, then I started rubbing her in earnest. Adrianna rolled her hips, fucking herself against my hand.

Her head was thrown back against the couch cushion, her eyes screwed shut as she reached for her release. I shifted slightly, taking a hunk of skin between my teeth, right at the ridge of her shoulder. I bit down, wanting to mark her, and moved my hand faster, stroking her fast and rough with the help of the fabric between her legs.

Suddenly Adrianna stiffened and then she was flying, making tiny whimpering noises as she rode the waves of her orgasm. As she came down, her eyes snapped open, wide and wondering.

"Holy fuck," she whispered. "That was incredible."

I couldn't help but give her a satisfied smile. "Wait until you see what I can do when you're naked."

Adrianna

The next week passed quickly. I couldn't stop thinking about what Erin and I did on her couch. The way she'd brought me to orgasm without even getting me naked. I didn't even know that was possible.

I'd wanted to return the favor, was desperate to touch more of her curvy body, but Erin had insisted that we wait.

"You need time to process this and decide if this is what you really want," she told me as she'd buttoned up her shirt, hiding those perfect breasts.

I was so distracted by the sight of them I could scarcely process her words. I'd seen women's breasts before of course, in movies or in passing at the gym. Whenever I'd encountered them I'd averted my eyes, not wanting to look like I was staring. Now I couldn't believe that I'd deprived myself of that sight for so many years.

I walked around in a horny daze, forcing myself to pay attention as I attended my classes. This semester I was taking the second in a three class series of introduction to business classes, the next level photography class with a different instructor, and two electives for my general degree, a writing class, and an art history class. I loved going to school, even if I was too old for all the fun activities people participated in when they were eighteen. It was good for me to challenge my brain and think about my plans for the future.

In between classes and homework I saw the counselor who'd helped me move past my relationship with my husband and volunteered at the domestic violence survivor shelter where I'd lived for a year, wanting to help other women in my situation and give back.

Even though I kept busy, Erin was never far from my mind. We texted multiple times a day, flirting and talking about what was happening in our lives. I knew that she had some concern about getting into a relationship with me, but I was all in. I just needed to prove it to her.

After a long conversation with my sister Jasmine, I decided to invite Erin out for a date. I already knew that Flora usually slept over at her grandparents' house on Saturdays so Erin could take catering shifts. When Erin said that she was working an early afternoon wedding, I suggested that we get together after. It was cliché, but I suggested a movie.

We met at one of those new restaurant theaters that were popping up over the city, the ones that were set up like you were watching a movie in your living room. As we settled down together on a cozy little love seat, a server came to take our dinner order. Erin told me about the wedding she'd worked at, and how the father of the bride got so drunk he fell onto a table of guests, upending plates and drinks and making a big mess.

"Apparently he doesn't like the groom," Erin told me. "He kept ranting that his daughter was making a big mistake."

It reminded me of my own wedding. When my father was walking me down the aisle he'd whispered, "It's not too late, Pumpkin. I can get you out of here. There's no shame in calling this off."

I'd laughed, playing it off like a joke, but now I realized he was giving me a warning, one I was too young and in love to heed. There was no sense in looking back though. I was resolved to leave the past behind me and embrace my future, whatever that would be. Hopefully, Erin would be a part of it.

Erin and I snuggled during the movie and once it was over, I invited her over to my house for a drink. She turned to me and gave me a smirk.

"I don't want a drink. I want dessert."

"Um, we can stop some place," I suggested. "Or I think I have some cookies somewhere."

Erin laughed and leaned closer, her breath ticking my ear. "I want to eat your pussy, Adrianna."

I gasped, and a rush of arousal flooded my panties.

"I'd like that too," I squeaked.

Erin's laugh was wicked as she sprung to her feet and grabbed my hand. "Let's go."

We raced back to my apartment, giggling like schoolgirls. As soon as we stepped inside my place we flew together, kissing each other like we'd been apart for years. When we finally pulled away, we were breathless.

Erin cupped my face in her hands and waited for me to meet her eyes.

"I want to fuck you, but if you're not ready, we can wait. I promise I won't be mad."

"I'll be mad if we wait any longer," I said, grabbing her hand. "Let's go to the bedroom."

Once we were in the bedroom, we made quick work of removing our clothes, standing before each other naked. My eyes raked over Erin's lush curves, my excitement ratcheting up even more. When I was with my husband I'd always been self-conscious about being naked, ready for him to criticize my every flaw, but with Erin I only saw desire. It was a heady experience.

Feeling bold, I sat on the bed and widened my legs. Erin's gaze went right to my pussy, and I was certain she could see how wet I was already.

"I believe you said something about dessert?" I teased.

She was on her knees in front of me in a flash, pulling my thighs over her shoulders. When she blew on the outside of my pussy I shivered in excitement. Finally, finally, she lowered her head, licking along my seam.

"You're already so wet for me," she whispered against my flesh.

Then she slid her tongue inside my folds, licking me up and down until I was writing against her face. Erin gripped my hips, holding me in place, licking and teasing until I was incoherent with lust. Her tongue slid up to my clitoris, tapping against my little bud while her fingers slid into my opening. One finger, then two, moving in and out slowly, then picking up speed.

I was overwhelmed with sensation, and when she crooked her fingers inside me, finding my G-spot, I detonated, giving into my orgasm with complete abandon. I shook and whined and gripped her head with my thighs so hard I was surprised I didn't tear off her head. And when it was over, all I could do was lay on the bed, panting for breath and smiling.

ERIN

I wiped Adrianna's juices off my mouth with the back of my hand, watching her carefully. Her legs had slipped off my shoulders, and she was spreadeagled on the edge of the bed, her face the very picture of bliss.

"That was my first orgasm with another person," she sighed. "Well, my first naked orgasm anyway."

My work here was done. I didn't need to get off tonight, I'd taken an immense amount of pleasure satisfying Adrianna.

"Let's do you now", Adrianna said, lifting her head.

Or maybe we weren't done.

Adrianna sat up, her gaze almost intense, not a bit of uncertainty or insecurity showing through.

"You said what gives me pleasure probably gives you pleasure too, right?"

I nodded.

"Well, that gave me a hell of a lot of pleasure. I want to taste you too, Erin. Can I?"

Like I could say no.

"I wouldn't mind that at all," I said mildly, even as my heart started thudding fast enough to make me lightheaded.

I got up on the bed, scooting towards the middle and pushing a pillow under my head. When Adrianna moved closer, I bent my knees, then slowly dropped them out to the side. Her eyes widened.

"I never thought of a woman's... that part of the body, as beautiful before," she said, her voice awed. "But I was wrong."

I giggled at her sudden attack of shyness.

"You mean a pussy?" I teased. "A vagina? Vag? Vajayjay? Coochie? Muff? Snatch?"

Adrianna burst out laughing. "Stop. For the love of God, stop before I change my mind about eating you out."

I cupped my breasts with my hands and widened my legs a little more. "Well, get on with it then."

At first she was tentative, her tongue moving slowly, barely skimming the surface of my vulva. But then Adrianna's tongue slipped between my pussy lips, and she became more confident, licking me from bottom to top.

"Does that feel okay?" she paused to ask.

"It feels good," I reassured her. "You can add more pressure."

She caught on fast, allowing me to relax against the mattress, enjoying the sensation. Adrianna used her fingers to spread me wider, licking me in earnest now. She circled around my clit a few times, then slid slower, pressing the tip of her tongue against my opening.

"Do it," I gasped, surprised at her boldness.

She pressed her tongue inside, licking in and out of me, making my heart thunder in my chest. It felt so good.

"Touch my clit," I ordered, pulling on her hair for emphasis.

She moved her fingers upward, teasing the swollen bundle of nerves with her fingers, then giving it a little pinch.

"Yes, that's it, I'm so close," I praised.

Her tongue started plundering me in earnest while her fingers continued to tease my clit. My hips were rolling now, and I ground against her face as I chased my release. Adrianna dug the fingers of her free hand into my hip, adding a bite of pain that helped send me over the edge.

"Ahh!" I wailed as a strong orgasm rolled through my body, electrifying every one of my nerve endings and emptying my mind of everything but the sensation of pleasure.

Adrianna continued to lick my pussy until the shaking stopped. Then she crawled her way up my body and gave me a hard kiss before flopping her head down on my shoulder with a satisfied sigh.

"That was super fun."

I lifted my head to stare at her. "I have to say, for a beginner you seemed to know your way around a woman's body."

She winced, her face turning bright red.

"What?" I asked.

"Do you promise not to make fun of me?" she asked.

"Um. I don't know, I guess?"

"Jasmine gave me a book on lesbian sex," she confessed in a rush. "I've been studying it. It has diagrams and technique suggestions. It was quite helpful."

I started laughing. "You studied how to have sex with me?"

"Well, I didn't want to get it wrong," she said, her voice small.

I sobered immediately, all the things she'd told me about her husband coming crashing back.

"Adrianna," I said, lifting her chin so she would look at me. "I'm teasing you, not mocking you. I know you didn't have a lot of experience with this in your marriage, but there's a difference between laughing *with* someone about something amusing and cruelly laughing *at* someone."

"Okay, sorry."

"Don't apologize," I said firmly. "I'm incredibly touched that you took the time to make sure that I didn't need to become your lesbian tutor. You just made me come my brains out, so take the win."

She gave me a smile. "Got it."

"One more thing…"

I waited for her to focus on me.

"After we recover, I want to see what else you learned in that book."

Adrianna

Six months later...

"I can't believe how fast this school year went," I said as I walked over to where Erin and Flora were waiting for me.

The mother and daughter had a year-end tradition: ice cream for dinner to celebrate a successful year. We met up at one of those ice cream places where you could add your own toppings, which Flora assured me was the best ice cream place in town.

"Remember our deal, Flora," Erin said. "You have to add at least two kinds of fruit to your sundae."

As Flora skipped off to check out her options, I nudged my shoulder against my girlfriend's.

"Do you really think that's going to cancel out all the sugar and fat?" I teased.

"Well, it can't hurt."

Erin threaded her fingers through mine.

"Come on, let's get our celebratory dinner, then we'll all collapse on the couch in a sugar coma."

The last six months had flown by. Erin and I were exclusively dating, and I spent a lot of time with both her and Flora. After a few weeks we'd eased Flora into the idea that her mother could have sleepovers with her friends just like she did, and Flora seemed oblivious to anything else going on. We were careful to only give each other a hug or a quick kiss on the cheek when we were around her.

We'd practiced everything in my book and then some. The passion still burned strong between us, but then again, so did our friendship. We could talk for hours, and despite our small age gap, I'd never felt so close to anyone before, other than my sister.

Jasmine was now in a relationship with her roommate Grace, something I could have predicted from the first time I saw them together. They were raising cats together and living their best life, and I couldn't be happier for them. About once a month or so Jasmine and I would set up a double date with our partners, and we all got along quite well. We'd even spent Easter together, the four of us plus Flora.

Now with summer coming up, I was going to help watch Flora two days a week. I was only taking two classes this summer, both of them on different days than Erin was teaching her classes. When I'd first suggested it, Erin had been resistant to the idea, not because she didn't think Flora and I would do well together, but because she was still stubbornly independent. I was working on that.

Little did she know that Flora and I had secret plans to figure out how to fix some things in the house, like the leaking faucet and the loose stair on the front porch. Erin's old house needed a lot of minor repairs that she never seemed to have time to address. We'd already started making a list of things that we wanted to tackle, with the help of YouTube of course.

Flora, Erin, and I piled up our bowls with ice cream and toppings, eating until we were all stuffed.

We were just walking out of the shop when I heard someone call my name, a voice that made my heart stop: my ex-husband. I took a deep breath to tamp down the shiver of fear, reminding myself that he had no power over me. I was safe now.

Don looked a little older than the last time I'd seen him, and a little weaker. Or maybe I'd just built him up as bigger and stronger than he really was. He was holding hands with a girl that looked to be barely out of her teens, a diamond ring on her finger.

I'd heard that he'd gotten remarried, but I hadn't heard she was so young. Then again, that's how he liked them – young and weak. I wondered if he was still fucking his assistant on the side.

Don stepped closer, his eyes raking over my body, a sneer forming as he silently told me that I'd come up lacking. I was ten pounds heavier than when we'd been together, and I'd added highlights to my hair. If we'd been alone and not in public, no doubt he'd tell me in detail how terrible I looked.

"Who's that, Miss Adrianna?" Flora asked, bringing me back to the present.

I straightened my spine and met Don's eye. "It's nobody. He's nobody."

His eyes flared with anger and the girl next to him gasped. I wanted to tell her to run away. I wanted to give her my card so when she was ready to leave him I could help her get into a shelter, but I knew this girl as well as I knew myself. She wouldn't hear it now. Wouldn't believe it. She needed to come to it herself. Hopefully, that would happen before she was seriously injured, because if there was one thing I'd learned about men like my ex-husband, it was that they all followed a pattern of escalating violence.

Erin pulled Flora a little bit behind her, no doubt connecting the dots. Silently dismissing my ex-husband, I looked down at my little friend and gave her a smile.

"Let's go home, sweetie."

I could feel Don staring after us as we walked away. It must be galling for him, knowing that despite him I was living my best life. There was no doubt looking at me with Erin and Flora that we were a family. Something I'd never had before.

We walked up the street to the car, then tucked Flora into the back seat. When Erin closed the door, I touched her shoulder, waiting for her to look at me.

"I love you," I said softly.

I'd never said it before. Neither of us had.

"I just want you to know."

Erin's mouth opened and closed a few times as she stared at me. My stomach dropped when she didn't say it back, even though I knew she loved me. If she wasn't ready to admit it, that was okay. Her silence didn't hurt – that much.

"Let's get you guys home," I said lightly, walking around the front of the car.

Erin slid into the passenger seat. "Adrianna..."

"It's fine, really," I said. "I didn't tell you so you could say it back. I just wanted you to know how I was feeling."

Flora chattered the entire way home, hyped up on her sugary dinner, giving Erin and me a reprieve from having to talk. When I pulled up in front of their house, Erin finally spoke to me.

"Are you staying over?"

Her voice sounded a little bit unsure, which was totally unlike her, but I was still reeling from everything that had happened since we left the ice cream shop. I needed some alone time to process how I was feeling.

"No, I'm heading home," I told her.

"Adrianna, please. Come inside."

I shook my head. "I need to be alone tonight."

I turned my head and gave Flora a smile. "I'll see you soon, okay Flora?"

The little girl looked between me and her mother, clearly sensing that something was happening, but not sure what. Erin got out of the car and opened the back door, reaching in to unbuckle Flora's belt.

"Come on Flora-bell, it's time for a bath. You have ice cream all over you."

Erin looked over at me. "Talk to you later?"

"Sure."

Erin

I felt like the biggest asshole in the world. We'd been having such a nice night, gorging ourselves on ice cream to celebrate the end of the school year. Then we'd seen *him*.

I'd known immediately that the man on the street was Adrianna's ex-husband. It was in the way she stiffened, then took a deep breath to calm herself. It was in the way he'd sneered at her and the way he'd barked out her name. But most of all, it was in the way the very young woman who'd been with him had flinched, closing in on herself like she was too afraid to breathe.

It was like coming face to face with a character out of a horror movie. I'd felt the strongest urge to grab both my girlfriend and my daughter and run away to get them to safety. Instead I'd just stood there, staring like an idiot.

Kind of the way I did when Adrianna told me that she loved me. I'd seen the flash of hurt in her eyes when I didn't respond. I hadn't meant to hurt her, I was just off-kilter. And the timing of her declaration of love right after seeing her ex-husband made me question it.

Now with the benefit of a good night's sleep, I realized that was unfair. Of course she loved me. I'd known it long before she ever vocalized it. And I loved her too. My love for her was bone-deep, but I'd kept it to myself, some small part of me remembering all the times I'd professed my love to a woman and then gotten dumped.

When we first got together I'd teased Adrianna that she needed a relationship tutor, but the truth was, I needed one just as badly. We'd muddled through together though and I hoped everything that happened last night hadn't messed it up for us.

I texted Adrianna to say good night before I went to bed, but she hadn't responded. After a short debate with myself, I texted her again while I was waiting for Flora to wake up.

MY NEW TEACHER

> **Erin:** *Good morning. How are you doing? Are you OK? I hope you're OK.*

A few minutes went by with no response, even though I could see that she'd read my message.

> **Erin:** *I'm sorry I reacted the way I did last night. I can't really explain it, but I'm glad you said what you said, because I love you too.*

> **Erin:** *Not that I meant to tell you that over text.*

> **Erin:** *Anyway, can we talk?*

I waited impatiently as the little dots appeared and disappeared on the phone, telling me that Adrianna was composing a response.

> **Adrianna:** *I'm fine. I just need some time alone. I have a lot of things to think about.*

> **Erin:** *We can think about them together. Please, don't pull away.*

> **Adrianna:** *I'm not pulling away, I'm just asking you for some space. Just*

> *for a couple of days. I'm not going anywhere, I promise.*

> **Erin: You'd better not.**

I didn't hear from Adrianna the rest of the day Friday, or at all over the weekend. I vacillated between panicking and telling myself I needed to respect her wishes in order for her to come back to me.

As usual, Flora spent Saturday night at my parents' house, and I worked a catering job for Gail. When I came home to my empty bed it nearly killed me. I'd gotten used to Saturday nights being our alone time, just me and Adrianna, the one day of the week where we could be as loud as we wanted having sex and didn't have to lock the door to prevent a nosy little eight year old from walking in on us.

I'd slept alone most of my life, but somehow I didn't remember how to do it anymore. I tossed and turned and stared at my phone, willing Adrianna to text me again.

By the time Monday came along, I was grumpy as hell. Grumpy enough that Flora called me out on it.

"Mommy, do you have a tummy ache?"

I looked up from staring into my coffee cup. "What? No, why?"

"You keep making a face like you have a tummy ache."

I gave my daughter a wry look. "It's my heart that aches, not my tummy."

"How come, Mommy?"

"Because I haven't seen Adrianna. I miss my friend."

Flora crossed her arms, giving me a look that clearly conveyed that I was an idiot.

"You can call her. You have her cell phone number."

I was considering taking my eight year old's advice when my phone beeped with a text. I jumped as I recognized Adrianna's ring tone. My heart was pounding so hard I could scarcely open up my message app.

> **Adrianna:** *Can you come over for dinner tonight at six? I was hoping we could talk.*

> **Erin:** *Yes. I'll see if my parents can watch Flora.*

> **Adrianna:** *That's okay, bring her along.*

I frowned at my phone. If she didn't mind having Flora there, we definitely weren't going to be making up. Not that we'd fought or anything, but it certainly felt like we had. Or maybe we were. I was so confused.

Surely she wasn't going to break up with me? Not in front of my daughter. My mind was spinning with questions, but instead I told her that Flora and I would see her at six.

"Hey Flora," I said. "That was Miss Adrianna. She invited us to come to her house for dinner tonight, what do you think?"

"I hope she makes her famous macaroni and cheese," Flora said. Adrianna made it at least twice a month for us and it was Flora's favorite thing. "Can you text her and ask her?"

"No, it's rude to make requests like that when you're invited to someone's house for dinner."

Flora considered my response for a moment before asking, "Does this mean your heart doesn't hurt anymore, Mommy?"

"I'm not sure."

Adrianna

The days away from Erin had been good, even if they were hard. I'd spent the weekend journaling and processing and after a good session with my therapist this morning, I was ready to jump back into my relationship with Erin. Assuming that she was okay with it, I mean. We hadn't broken up or even had a fight.

I'd only asked for a few days of space, surely she could understand why seeing my ex-husband had thrown me for a loop? It was why I'd confessed my true feelings for her although in retrospect, maybe it had been too soon. For all her confidence, Erin wasn't that different from me. Sure, she had more dating experience, but it was so long ago it hardly counted. It was hard for her to open up and share.

We'd both been burned, but what we had now was good. I was willing to fight for it if she was.

When I heard the knock on my door I damn near jumped out of my skin. Time to execute my plan. I opened the door, smiling as Flora rushed in, throwing her arms around my waist and damn near knocking me over. She was growing by the day.

"Hi Flora!"

"Miss Adrianna I missed you!"

"I just saw you Thursday," I reminded her. "Today's Monday. It's only been four days."

"That's way too long," she said dramatically.

She let me go and I pulled Erin in for a quick hug. Her eyes searched mine and she gave me a tremulous smile. Before either of us could speak, Flora interjected.

"Are we havin' macaroni and cheese for dinner?" she asked.

I couldn't help but laugh. The little girl was a big fan of my homemade mac and cheese recipe. "Kind of."

Flora looked up with a confused frown. "What does that mean?"

Just then there was a knock on the door. Flora and Erin stepped back and I opened up for my sister Jasmine and her girlfriend Grace. Flora gave them each a hug. She was a big fan of the couple – and their cats.

Erin sent me a questioning look, but I just smiled.

"Flora, Grace and I were hoping you could help us with something," Jasmine said.

"What?" Flora asked, her tone super serious.

"Well, our kittens are lonely. We were hoping you could come to visit them. We thought maybe we could all make a fort in the living room, watch movies, and have a sleep-over."

Flora's eyes grew huge. "With the kittens?"

Jasmine nodded and I looked over to Erin to make sure she was okay with it. My sister and Grace had babysat for Flora a few times when we went on a date night, so I figured she'd be okay with the plan. Erin nodded.

"I even made you a pan of mac and cheese to take with you and share, Flora."

Flora turned to her mother.

"Can I go Mommy? Please? The kittens need me."

"You have to be a good girl then," Erin said sternly. "You listen to all of Miss Jasmine and Miss Grace's instructions. No whining or arguing. And be gentle with the kittens."

"I know Mommy," Flora said impatiently. "I'm not a baby, you know."

I smothered a smile. It was the same conversation they had every time Flora went to stay with someone else.

"Okay, I'll go get your mac and cheese so you can go help the kittens."

Erin followed them out so they could put Flora's booster seat in the back of Jasmine's car. Meanwhile I set the table to get ready for our romantic dinner. By the time Erin returned I had a bottle of wine open and breathing, candles lit on the table, and I was at the stove getting the rest of dinner ready to go.

Erin walked up behind me, wrapping her arms around my waist, and pressing a quick kiss to my neck.

"This all looks romantic."

"I wanted to do something nice for you," I said, turning into her embrace. "To thank you for giving me the space that I needed."

"And was the space helpful?"

"Yeah, I had some stuff to process. I'm not going to lie, seeing Don threw me for a loop." I paused. "No, that's not right, seeing that young girl with him threw me for a loop."

She nodded. "I understand."

We stared at each other for a long moment. "Any chance you saved some of that mac and cheese for us?" she asked.

I laughed. "Yeah. We're having baked chicken, asparagus, and salad, with a side of mac and cheese."

"See? This is why I love you."

She looked a little surprised at her own words. I tilted my head and waited.

"I do love you, Adrianna. I was thrown off when you said it the other night, especially because you'd just seen your asshole ex. I was worried it was, I don't, reflexive or something."

I started to respond but she held up her hand to stop me. "After I had some time to think about it, I realized that was ridiculous. I knew you loved me, even if you never said it, just like hopefully you knew I loved you."

Erin

"I was pretty sure that you did," Adrianna said. "But in the end, it's more about showing love than just words. I think we both know that words can be empty."

"Yeah."

"Now how about we eat dinner and catch up on what we missed the last few days," she suggested. "We have the whole night ahead of us."

We sat in the dimly lit dining room, smiling at each other over the flickering candles, talking and eating our dinner. It was such a perfect moment that I couldn't help the next words that came out of my mouth.

"Move in with me. Well, me and Flora."

Adrianna's head reared back in surprise. "Where did this come from?"

I scooted over to the chair next to her and grabbed her hand. "I was just thinking about how perfectly matched we are and how much I enjoy just *being* with you. It made me think, we could be doing this every night."

A series of emotions passed across Adrianna's face as she considered my words.

"We've only been together six months," she said. "Isn't it too soon?"

I placed my hand on her chest, over her beating heart. "What does your heart say?"

"My heart says I've made bad decisions before."

"If you move in with us, it will be the best bad decision you ever made, I guarantee it."

Adrianna burst out laughing. "You're crazy, do you know that?"

I nodded. "Crazy for you."

She stared at me for a long moment. "Are you sure?"

"I've never been surer about anything in my life, other than my decision to have Flora."

"Okay then, well my lease is up in two months, how about we do it then?"

I couldn't help the huge smile that broke out on my face. "That sounds great."

Adrianna stood up and grabbed my hand.

"I have a surprise for you."

"Is it mac and cheese?" I teased.

"Better."

Leaving all the dishes on the table, Adrianna led me into the bedroom. She had a ton of candles lit all around the room, each of them in glass containers for safety. She whipped her shirt over her head and dropped her jeans, revealing a white lace teddy that hugged her curves. I nearly swallowed my tongue.

"That's hot as fuck," I said, moving closer.

She stepped back and shook her head.

"You're going to take off your clothes," she said, hopping onto the bed and settling onto her back. "Then you're going to hop on up and I'm going to lick your pussy until you're screaming my name."

"I'm on board with this plan," I said, quickly removing my clothes.

I crawled up the bed, pressing kisses along her body on the way, then kneeled on either side of Adrianna's head and grabbed the headboard. She reached up and tugged on my hips, encouraging me to lower down on her face.

I cried out with the first touch of her wet tongue on the outside of my pussy.

"I haven't even gone inside yet," she laughed from between my legs.

I made an impatient noise that had her laughing again.

"Okay baby, hold on, I've got you."

Using her fingers to spread my lower lips, she licked me from top to bottom, her movements slow and leisurely. Up and down, up and down, she repeated the motion until I was writhing on top of her, desperate for more.

"Please," I gasped. "Adrianna."

Her tongue slid into my opening, fucking me with it while I ground into her face. I was too far gone to worry about if I was smothering her, though I couldn't help but remember what she told me the first time we'd done this.

"If you smother me, I'll die happy."

Adrianna slid one hand upwards, catching my clitoris between her fingers, rubbing and pinching until I was ready to explode. As if she knew, she shifted her head enough to order, "Come for me now, Erin."

It was like she'd shot a starter gun. I rocked my hips and cried out her name as my release rolled through my body. Adrianna licked and sucked and hummed against my pussy as I gave myself over to the pleasure. When it finally abated, I was boneless. I dropped over to the side of the bed in a heap, panting.

Adrianna rolled over to face me, her expression showing that she was proud of herself.

"I think I blacked out for a minute," I told her shakily. "That was incredible."

She pulled me into her arms and pressed a kiss on my forehead. "Every time gets better and better."

"If you let me love you," I told her solemnly. "I promise that will continue for the rest of our lives."

"Well, it's lucky for you that I plan to let you love me, as long as you'll let me love you back."

"Would it be bad if I asked for more mac and cheese before we do that again?" I asked. "I know I was just sitting there but I think I burned a lot of calories. You can wear that teddy."

Epilogue – Adrianna

Two years later...

"Are you both ready for the first day of school?" I asked as Erin and Flora came into the kitchen.

"You cooked?" Erin asked, looking pleased.

"Yes, I made you two my special first day of school breakfast sandwiches."

"Are they different than your regular breakfast sandwiches?" Flora asked.

She'd just turned ten and was growing up way faster than either Erin or I wanted.

"Yes," I said solemnly. "They have twice as much bacon."

Erin rolled her eyes. She was on a quest to get Flora and me to eat healthier. My girl and I both loved three food groups: carbs, ice cream, and bacon.

"Don't worry, I added some spinach and tomato," I told Erin, sending Flora a wink.

"What are you going to do today while we're gone?" Erin asked.

"Well, I'm going to take that little guy for a walk," I said, pointing at our sweet but chunky pit bull.

As usual, Brutus was sleeping. We'd adopted him from a rescue when he was two years old and even though he was only four now, he acted like an old man. If I let him get away with it, he'd spend ninety percent of his time sleeping and ten percent eating. He was the laziest dog ever, but we all loved him anyway.

"Then I'm going into the studio to work on some film."

I'd finished my photography training and had opened a small studio. I specialized in family portraits and graduation photos, but I also worked the occasional wedding or party. It wasn't a career that was going to make me rich, but I did okay, and I was starting to build up a clientele.

Erin had finally gotten a full-time faculty member position in the arts department at the college which meant better pay, better benefits, and weekends free to hang out with me and Flora. We both knew that eventually Flora would become a teenager and not want to spend so much time with her two moms, so we were snapping up all the time we could with her now while she was young.

I handed them both the lunches I'd packed. Erin and I split up the household duties equally, but I did most of the cooking and food preparation, partly because I enjoyed it and partly because I was so much better at it. That was okay though, Erin had other skills.

"Have a good day Flora," I said, kissing her forehead.

"And you too, baby," I said, moving to kiss Erin too.

She pulled my head down to give me a proper kiss, earning a groan of disgust from Flora who hated it when we did "disgusting kissy stuff."

As I watched my girls head off to school, I couldn't help but think about how much richer my life was now. When I was with my ex-husband I'd dreamed of having a kid and a dog and someone to come home to, and with Erin, I'd finally gotten exactly what I always wanted.

***

Read about how Adrianna's sister Jasmine found her girlfriend Grace in *"My Broken Heart"* available now at https://books2read.com/MyBroken.

You can find more of Reba's lesbian romances at *Books2read.com/rl/lesbianromance*

If you liked this book, please consider leaving a review or rating to let me know.

Keep reading for a special preview of Reba Bale's lesbian romance "The Divorcee's First Time".

Be sure to join my newsletter for more great books. You'll receive a free book when you join my newsletter. Subscribers are the first to hear about all of my new releases and sales. Visit my mailing list sign-up at https://books.rebabale.com/lesbianromance to download your free book today.

SPECIAL PREVIEW OF THE DIVORCEE'S FIRST TIME

A CONTEMPORARY LESBIAN ROMANCE BY REBA BALE

"It's done," I said triumphantly. "My divorce is final."

My best friend Susan paused in the process of sliding into the restaurant booth, her sharply manicured eyebrows raising almost to her hairline. "Dickhead finally signed the papers?" she asked, her tone hopeful.

I nodded as Susan settled into the seat across from me. "The judge signed off on it today. Apparently his barely legal girlfriend is knocked up, and she wants to get a ring on her finger before the big event." I explained with a touch of irony in my voice. "The child bride finally got it done for me."

Susan smiled and nodded. "Well congratulations and good riddance. Let's order some wine."

We were most of the way through our second bottle when the conversation turned back to my ex. "I wonder if Dickhead and his Child Bride will last for the long haul," Susan mused.

I shook my head and blew a chunk of hair away from my mouth.

"I doubt it," I told her. "Someday she's gonna roll over and think, there's got to be something better out there than a self-absorbed man child who doesn't know a clitoris from a doorknob."

Susan laughed, sputtering her wine. I eyed her across the table. Although she was ten years older than me, we had been best friends for the last five years. We worked together at the accounting firm. She had been my trainer when I first came there, fresh out of school with my degree. We bonded over work, but soon realized that we were kindred spirits.

Susan was rapidly approaching forty but could easily pass for my age. Her hair was black and shiny, hinting at her Puerto Rican heritage, with blunt bangs and blond highlights that she paid a fortune for. Her face was clear and unlined, with large brown eyes and cheek bones that could cut glass. She was an avid runner and worked hard to maintain a slim physique since the women in her family ran towards the chunkier side.

I was almost her complete opposite. Blonde curls to her straight dark hair, blue eyes instead of brown, curvy where she was lean, introverted to her extrovert.

But somehow, we clicked. We were closer than sisters. Honestly, I don't know how I would have gotten through the last year without her. She had been the first one I called when my marriage fell apart, and she had supported me throughout the whole process.

It had been a big shock when I came home early one day and found my husband getting a blow job in the middle of our living room. It had been even more shocking when I saw the fresh young face at the other end of that blow job.

"What the fuck are you doing?" I had screeched, startling them both out of their sex stupor. "You're getting blow jobs from children now?"

The girl had looked up from her knees with eyes glowing in righteous indignation. "I'm not a child, I'm nineteen," she had informed me proudly. "I'm glad you finally found out. I give him what you don't, and he loves me."

I looked into the familiar eyes of my husband and saw the panic and confusion there. I made it easy for him. "Get out," I told him firmly, my voice leaving no room for argument. "Take your teenage girlfriend and get the fuck out. We're getting a divorce. Expect to hear from my lawyer."

The condo was in my name. I had purchased it before we were married, and since I had never added his name to the deed, he had no rights to it. There was no question he would be the one leaving.

My husband just stared at me with his jaw hanging open like he couldn't believe it. "But Jennifer," he whined. "You don't understand. Let me explain."

"There's nothing to understand," I told him sadly. "This is a deal breaker for me, and you know that as well as I do. We are done."

The girl had taken his hand and smiled triumphantly. "Come on baby," she told him. "Zip up and let's get out of here. We can finally be together like we planned."

"Yeah baby," I had sneered. "I'll box up your stuff. It'll be in the hallway tomorrow. Pick it up by six o'clock or I'm trashing it all."

After they left my first call was to the locksmith, but my second call was to Susan.

That night was the last time I had seen my husband until we had met for the court-ordered pre-divorce mediation. He spent most of that session reiterating what he had told me in numerous voice mails, emails and sessions spent yelling on the other side of my front door. He loved me. He had made a terrible mistake. He wasn't going to sign the papers. We were meant to be together. Needless to say, mediation hadn't been very successful. Fortunately, I had been careful to keep our assets separate, as if I knew that someday I would be in this situation.

Through it all, Susan had been my rock. In the end I don't think I was even that sad about the divorce, I was really angrier with myself for staying in a relationship that wasn't fulfilling with a man I didn't love anymore.

"You need to get some quality sex." Susan drew my attention back to the present. "Bang him out of your system."

"I don't know," I answered slowly. "I think I need a hiatus."

"A hiatus from what?" Susan asked with a frown. "You haven't had sex in what, eighteen months?"

I nodded. "Yeah, but I just can't take a disappointing fumble right now. I would rather have nothing than another three-pump chump."

I shook my head and continued, "I'm going to stick with my battery-operated boyfriend, he never disappoints me."

Susan smiled. "That's because you know your way around your own vajayjay."

She motioned to the waiter to bring us a third bottle of wine.

"That's why I like to date women," she continued. "We already know our way around the equipment."

I nodded thoughtfully. "You make a good point."

Susan leaned forward. "We've never talked about this," she said earnestly. "Have you ever been with a woman?"

For more of the story, check out "The Divorcee's First Time" by Reba Bale, available for immediate download at https://books2read.com/Divorcee.

***

Want a free book? Join my newsletter and a special gift. I'll contact you a few times a month with story updates, new releases, and special sales. Visit bit.ly/RebaBaleSapphic for more information.

OTHER BOOKS BY REBA BALE

Check out my other books, available on most major online retailers now. Go to at bit.ly/AuthorRebaBale to learn more.

Friends to Lovers Lesbian Romance Series

The Divorcee's First Time

My BFF's Sister

My Rockstar Assistant

My College Crush

My Fake Girlfriend

My Secret Crush

My Holiday Love

My Valentine's Gift

My Spring Fling

My Forbidden Love

My Office Wife

My Second Chance

Coming Out in Ten Dates

Worth Waiting For

My Party Planner

My Broken Heart

My New Teacher

The Surrender Club Lesbian Romance Series

Jaded

Hated

Fated

Saved

Caged

Dared

The Sapphic Security Series

Guarding the Senator's Daughter

Guarding the Rock Star

Guarding the Witness

Guarding the Billionaire

Playing to Win Lesbian Sports Series

Tumbling for Love

Racing for Love

Spiking for Love

The Second Chances Lesbian Romance Series

Last Christmas

The Summer I Fell in Love

Snowed in With You

My Kind of Girl

Menage Romances

Pie Promises

Tornado Warning

Summer in Paradise

Life of the Mardi

Bases Loaded

Two for One Deal

Penalty Box

Rock My Heart

The Unexpectedly Mine Series

Sinful Desires

Taken by Surprise

Just One Night

Forbidden Desires

Spanking & Sprinkles

Hotwife Erotic Romances

Hotwife in the Woods

Hotwife on the Beach

Hotwife Under the Tree

A Hotwife's Retreat

Hot Wife Happy Life

__Want a free book? Just join my newsletter at https://books.rebabale.com/lesbian. You'll be the first to hear about new releases, special sales, and free offers.__

ABOUT REBA BALE

Reba Bale writes erotic romance, lesbian romance, menage romance, & the spicy stories you want to read on a cold winter's night.

She lives in the Northwest with her family and two very spoiled dogs. When Reba is not writing she is reading the same naughty stories she likes to write.

For all of Reba's stories visit her webpage at https://books2read.com/rebabale.

You can also follow Reba on Ream and Medium for free stories, bonus epilogues and more. You can hear all about new releases and special sales by joining Reba's mailing list at **https://books.rebabale.com/lesbianromance**

Printed in Dunstable, United Kingdom